O'SULLIVAN STEW

A Tale Cooked Up In Ireland

By

HUDSON TALBOTT

PUFFIN BOOKS

This book is dedicated to the people of Ireland,
with gratitude for all they've given
to the rest of us.

PUFFIN BOOKS
Published by the Penguin Group
Penguin Putnam Books for Young Readers, 345 Hudson Street, New York, New York 10014, U.S.A.
Penguin Books Ltd, 27 Wrights Lane, London W8 5TZ, England
Penguin Books Australia Ltd, Ringwood, Victoria, Australia
Penguin Books Canada Ltd, 10 Alcorn Avenue, Toronto, Ontario, Canada M4V 3B2
Penguin Books (N.Z.) Ltd, 182-190 Wairau Road, Auckland 10, New Zealand
Penguin Books Ltd, Registered Offices: Harmondsworth, Middlesex, England

First published in the United States of America by G. P. Putnam's Sons, a division of Penguin Putnam Books for Young Readers, 1999
Published by Puffin Books, a division of Penguin Putnam Books for Young Readers, 2001

11 13 15 17 19 20 18 16 14 12

Copyright © Hudson Talbott, 1999
All rights reserved

THE LIBRARY OF CONGRESS HAS CATALOGED THE G. P. PUTNAM'S SONS EDITION AS FOLLOWS:
Talbott, Hudson. O'Sullivan stew / Hudson Talbott.   p.   cm.
Summary: When the witch of Crookhaven, a village on the zigzagging coast of Ireland, has her horse stolen by
the King and strikes back with famine and disaster, Kate decides to save the day by getting the horse back for her.
[1. Witchcraft—Fiction. 2. Horses—Fiction. 3. Ireland—Fiction.] I. Title. PZ7.T1530s 1999 [Fic]—dc21 98-5721 CIP AC

This edition ISBN 978-0-698-11889-8

Printed in the United States of America

Down along the zigzagging coast of Ireland, on the rocks of the very last zag, sat Kate O'Sullivan, daydreaming. She lived in nearby Crookhaven and came here every day to gather periwinkles for the evening stew. This was also the best spot to see the wild red stallion who sometimes thundered past on the shore. Kate was lost in her thoughts of him when suddenly a screeching voice shattered the peace.

"Let go of that horse or you'll all be toads by nightfall!"

Down the beach, the stallion was bucking and kicking furiously as soldiers tried to capture him.

"Let go of my horse, I say!" screeched an old woman, swinging her cane at the men. They just laughed at her.

"Crookhaven must pay its share of taxes to the king, madam," hissed the royal tax collector. "The horse will do nicely. His Majesty is fond of redheads."

"The good lads of Crookhaven won't stand for this!" the old woman shot back. Then she noticed Kate. "Run, child! Get help!"

Kate ran straight to the village square.

"Quick, everyone!" she called out. "The witch is in trouble! The king's soldiers are taking her horse!"

The folks stared at Kate for a moment, then went back to their chores.

She grabbed old Murphy's arm. "Didn't you hear me?" she shouted. "Our witch needs our help!"

"What do you mean, *our* witch?" he asked with a shrug. "She's not one of us. Let go of my sleeve."

"Murphy's right, ya know," added Flynn the sod cutter. "Who are we against the likes of them? She's a witch, after all. Let her fend for herself."

The villagers skulked into their homes, closing doors and shutters behind them. Kate took a deep breath and returned to face the witch alone.

"They were too BUSY?" the witch shrieked at Kate. "They're never too busy when they need a cure for a fever or a hex on their pests or a love potion! *Not one of us,* indeed!"

The old woman hobbled toward her door, then turned to Kate. "Save those periwinkles, child," she said. "You may need them."

It was a black day indeed when Crookhaven's witch
went into a snit. The fishnets came up empty. The cows
stopped giving milk. Gardens died. Trees fell on houses
with remarkable accuracy. And the rain was heavier
than usual. Desperate townsfolk went to the
witch to beg for mercy but were met by
a sign on her gate...

DON'T BOTHER—
I'm not "one of us"

Hungry days turned into starving weeks. But
just when Kate was thinking about boiling up her right
shoe, she had an idea.

"I've got it!" she announced to her brothers and father. "We'll steal back the horse and bring it to the witch. That'll make her happy!"

"The likes of us? Horse thieves?" cried her brother Fergus.

"Stealin' from the king?" asked Kelly, the other one.

"Ah, the poor little thing," said her father, Seamus, patting her on the cheek. "She's lost her wits from hunger."

"We've more than that to lose if we sit here and do nothing, Da!" said Kate. "But we've nothing to lose for trying."

The O'Sullivan men scratched their heads.

"Look at it this way. We're facing death in either case," she continued. "By the hangman's rope or the empty plate. Which way do your prefer to go?"

They scratched their heads again.

"You with me, then, lads?" she asked.

Kate O'Sullivan was known for her way with words.

And so the O'Sullivans found themselves on a quest to save Crookhaven.

They hiked for days until, at last, the king's mighty castle rose before them. The weary travelers found a hiding place to rest till midnight and to enjoy their last crusts of bread. Seamus took out his flask of home-brewed stout and squeezed hard for the very last drop. And what a fateful drop it was.

The O'Sullivans had many skills, but horse thieving was not one of them. Poor Seamus lost control and...

Guards came running from all directions. Soon the whole castle was awake and the O'Sullivans were thrown in front of the king himself.

"Well...Seamus O'Sullivan," said the king, "you don't look like a horse thief. But that doesn't mean you shouldn't hang like one. What have you to say for yourself?"

"Wuh-wuh well, uh-ur, Your Maj-jaj-aj..." Seamus babbled. He was trembling too hard to speak.

"You don't *talk* too well, either," said the king. He stared at Seamus for a long moment. Then his face darkened and his voice grew fierce. "Do you even realize the trouble you're in? Have you ever been in a worse spot in your life?"

Poor Seamus only trembled harder.

"*I* have," said a voice from the side. All eyes turned toward Kate. "It was the time I almost married the king of the leprechauns and was about to vanish into the Enchanted Realm forever. Oh, that was surely a closer call than this."

The king looked puzzled. "So, what happened?" he asked.

"Oh, I was only answering Your Majesty's question," Kate said softly. "I'd be delighted to tell you my story, but I have a small request if I do."

The king nodded, and Kate continued.

"If you agree that I was in a worse spot there than I am now, will you let us go free?"

"You dare to bargain with me?" thundered the king. He paced back and forth. "All right, then," he finally said. "I shall let you *alone* go free. But only if I like your story. It better be good."

"Well, Your Lordship, I had always been warned to beware on Midsummer's Eve. Weird things can happen. People can disappear forever. So I was hurrying home after milking Jasmine, late in the afternoon of that dreadful day, when a strange sleep overtook me. Try as I might to resist, I had no power against it."

"I awoke to find myself bound up with cobwebs like a mummy. Tiny fairy hands were carrying me through the fields and into the forest. We flew through the night until we reached a great clearing. There in the moonlight stood the king of the leprechauns himself, with all his grand and glorious company. The leader of the fairies came forward to greet him. A war between the fairies and the leprechauns was being settled, and the fairies presented me as a peace offering. They hoped I might be useful to the king, but he took one look at me and fell madly in love! He wanted to marry me that very night. With a clap of his hands, the wee folk set to work preparing a grand wedding banquet."

Now *that* was a party I'll not soon forget. The whole forest was dancing that night! And the music! It would've made the angels do a jig!

"Finally the moment came for the wedding to begin. Tiny fairy children flitted all around, showering me with golden fairy dust. I began to rise dreamily upward, when suddenly…

Bless you
Bless you
Bless you!
use your handkerchief!
Bless you!
Bless you
BLESS Y
Bless you!
Bless you!
Bless you!
Bless you
Bless you!
Bless you!
Bless you!

"In the blink of an eye, the wedding party had vanished. I could hear the wee folk but could no longer see them. My giant sneeze had blown away the veil of enchantment for a moment, giving me a chance to escape. I ran out of the forest and all the way home. My brothers were shocked to see me, but not half as much as I was to see them. They had grown taller than me overnight! Then it sank in: While I was spending one Midsummer's Night with the fairyfolk, five human years had passed. You see, Your Majesty, Fergus and Kelly are actually my *younger* brothers. But if I hadn't sneezed from the fairy dust, I wouldn't have seen them—or anyone—ever again.

"Now wouldn't you say that is a worse spot to be in than this?"

"Indeed I would, lass," said the king, "and you've earned your freedom. Now go."

"But if I go now, you'll miss the story of how Fergus was almost eaten by a sea serpent. Now *that* was a far worse spot to be in," said Kate. "But if you want me to go..."

"Wait, wait," said the king. "Worse than now?"

"You'll free him if you agree that it was?" asked Kate.

"Very well," said the king grumpily, "but it better be good."

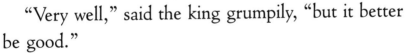

"Well, Your Highness, we fisherfolk know when the skies warn us to come ashore. But one day, just as a great storm was blowin' up and Fergus had just made it in, what do we see but a lovely young lass dive into the crashing waves! Quick as a flash, Fergus threw his boat back into the water and rowed out to save her.

"But the lad had no luck. For days the storm tossed him about like a pebble on a shaking blanket. When the seas finally calmed, he found himself drifting toward a small island. Or so he thought."

"'Ah! Company! Just in time for lunch!' bellowed an enormous serpent. 'You look like you haven't had a bite in days. Well, lad, I can fix that. I just love having drop-in guests! I'll open wide, and you drop in!'

"'But you'll be missing the best part!' called a nearby seal. 'Eating a fisherman without his boat is like eating a pie without its crust. It's nothing without that crunchy texture.'

"'You're right!' said the monster. 'Fisherman pie! Yum!'

"But as soon as the greedy beast started working his mouth around one end of the boat, the seal shoved the other end in, wedging the monster's jaws open."

"Fergus popped out of the boat and plunged into the water. Then the seal scooped him onto her back and carried him home to Crookhaven.

"I was on the beach when the seal brought Fergus back. And I tell you, I wouldn't believe it if I hadn't seen it with my own eyes, but when they came ashore, the seal turned into the girl he had tried to rescue! She kissed my poor half-dead brother, waved to me, and dove back into the sea.

"Now, Your Majesty, would you not agree that being in the jaws of a sea monster is a worse spot than where Fergus is right now?" asked Kate.

"I would, Miss O'Sullivan," said the king with a smile. "And he's lucky to have you, for he is now free. But someone must pay for the crime of…"

"Of course, Your Lordliness, but that someone surely isn't Kelly," said Kate. "His worse spot is far worse than ours! Almost torn to shreds by wild beasts, he was!"

"Wild beasts, you say?" asked the king, leaning forward.

Kate nodded but said nothing.

"Well, get on with it!" said the king.

Kate cleared her throat.

"Kelly has a way with animals, Your Majesty. One night, when he was on his way to market with a pig and a cow, he took shelter in an old barn and built a little fire. But he wasn't alone for long."

"In the firelight, Kelly could see the gleam of dozens of demonic cats' eyes. These weren't just *any* strays, mind you. Some were the size of tigers. One by one, they began to purr and lick their lips. The purring rose into rumbles, then howls, screeches, and finally an ear-splitting version of 'Danny Boy.' Poor Kelly thought he would go deaf before the end came.

"Their leader ambled out of the darkness—a huge, scruffy beast with one eye missing and teeth like daggers.

"'Now that we've sung for our supper, lad, what will you give us?' he snarled.

"'I haven't anything, except that pig,' said Kelly. 'He isn't...' Before Kelly finished the sentence, the cats finished the pig.

"'How about another tune?' asked the leader. With that, they launched into torturing 'Sweet Molly Malone.'

"'Now what will you give us?' he asked Kelly.

"'I have only the cow,' he said, 'and she's in rough shape!'

"But the cats were happy to polish her off.

"'And now, for dessert, "When Irish Eyes Are Smiling"!' But by the last stanza, Kelly was gone.

"'After him!' screeched the leader.

"They chased him through the woods until he came to a cliff and dashed up a tree.

"'He'll knife us one by one if we go up,' said the leader. 'Let's gnaw it down, lads!'

"Poor Kelly was howling so loud from fright that a wolf in the distance howled back. Then another and another. Soon a pack of wolves gathered on the cliff across the gorge. The cats hissed at the sight of them, but then laughed when they saw that the wolves couldn't get them."

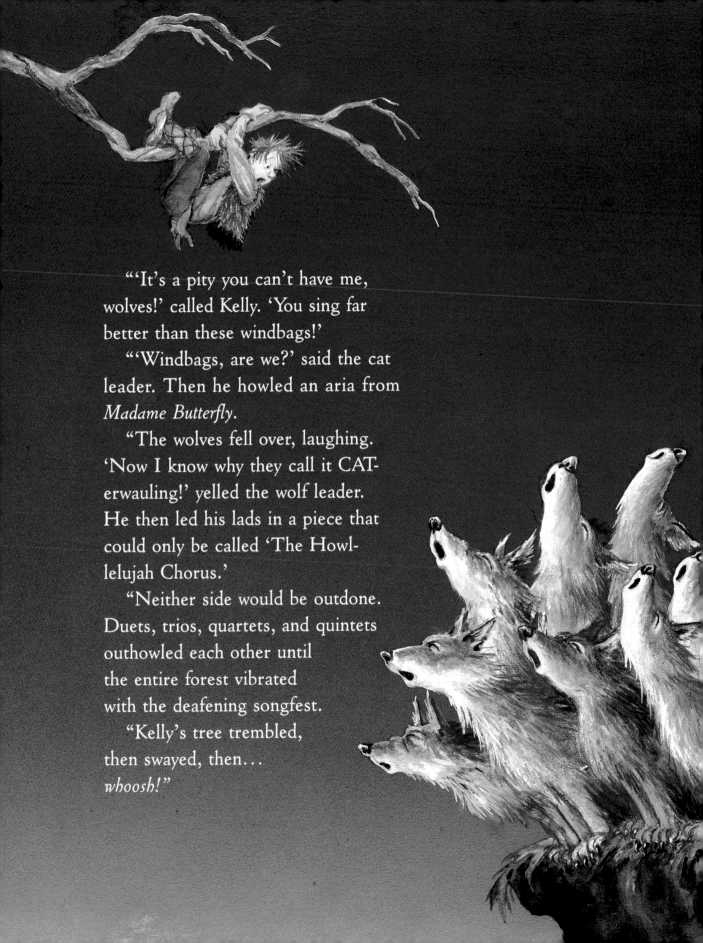

"'It's a pity you can't have me, wolves!' called Kelly. 'You sing far better than these windbags!'

"'Windbags, are we?' said the cat leader. Then he howled an aria from *Madame Butterfly*.

"The wolves fell over, laughing. 'Now I know why they call it CAT-erwauling!' yelled the wolf leader. He then led his lads in a piece that could only be called 'The Howl-lelujah Chorus.'

"Neither side would be outdone. Duets, trios, quartets, and quintets outhowled each other until the entire forest vibrated with the deafening songfest.

"Kelly's tree trembled, then swayed, then... *whoosh!*"

"A blizzard of fur filled the air as the enemies flew at each other on the fallen tree. Cats and wolves were whizzing by Kelly in all directions.

"Kelly clung to the tree until, at last, the forest was silent and he was safe. He gathered all the fur on the ground and brought it home," said Kate. "I spun it into yarn and dyed it kelly green.

"What do you think of my shawl, Your Majesty?"

"As lovely as you, Miss O'Sullivan," said the king. "And before you ask, yes, Kelly is free. But your father must pay for the crime. After all, he's the one who should have known better."

"Oh, you needn't tell me, Your Lordship. I'm the one who must look after him!" said Kate. "He was even wilder as a youth, beating up that giant and all. I never know what he'll do next."

"*He* beat up a giant?" asked the king.

"To save a baby's life!" said Kate. "He just laughs at danger."

"Tell us the story, and then we'll see who's laughing… and who's still trembling," said the king. Kate nodded.

"One day, very long ago, when my father, Seamus, was out boating, he came upon an enchanted isle. It was a place of unearthly beauty, but Seamus could hear someone crying somewhere."

"He followed the sound until he fell into a deep ravine. At the bottom was a tearful young mother with her baby. She told Seamus that they were captives of a giant who had ordered her to prepare her child for the giant's dinner.

"A moment later, the giant's ladder slid into the ravine and two huge feet came stomping down the rungs. Seamus told the woman to hide the child. Then he jumped into the stewpot himself."

"'I'm hungry enough to eat a horse!' growled the giant. 'But I better stick with baby tonight. I'm watching my weight.' He looked into the stewpot and smiled at Seamus simmering away. 'What a chubby little devil! But those look like whiskers. Red chin-whiskers!'

"'He's very mature for his age,' said the mother, sliding the lid back on the pot. 'Why don't you go lie down? I'll call you when dinner's ready.'

"The giant was snoring in no time. Seamus, now red as a lobster, slipped out of the pot, tied on the baby's bonnet, and scrunched up on a platter in the middle of the table. The woman covered him with stew and stuck an apple in his mouth. Then she lit the candles, pulled out the huge chair, and woke the giant.

"'Yummmmyyy!' he exclaimed, picking up the platter."

"Just as the giant was about to gulp him down, Seamus spit the apple squarely into his huge eye. With that, the mother dumped the stewpot onto his enormous foot. While the giant leaped around blindly, howling in pain, Seamus and the mother and baby scrambled up the ladder. They dashed to the boat and rowed for their lives.

"As they reached their home shore, the young mother thanked Seamus for saving her child and herself. She wanted to reward him, but Seamus said hearing the child's laughter was reward enough. He waved farewell to them and took a dip in the cool water to soothe his burned skin.

"So, Your Majesty, I put it to you for the last time," said Kate. "Would you not agree that being in a giant's stew is a worse spot than where we are right now?"

The king looked glum. "I'd like to agree," he said slowly, "if only I could. But you've pushed me too far with this tale about your father. I am tempted to reward you simply for your vivid imagination. But really, Miss O'Sullivan, who in the world would ever believe such a far-fetched story about *him*?"

"I would," called a woman from the rear of the hall.
"Mother?" said the king. "What are you doing here?"
The queen mother made her way through the crowd
and went directly toward Seamus.

"At last, we meet again, kind sir!" she said, holding out her hand to Seamus. "I've waited so long to thank you properly for saving us. I've never told my son of that terrible time. But none of us would be here were it not for you."

The king was speechless.

"It's true," said the queen mother, turning to her son. "There is no cause for *hanging* this man, but for *honoring* him. We owe him our lives! And anything else he wants."

"How about the horse?" suggested Kate.

"That is the least we'll do, my dear Miss O'Sullivan!"
said the king. "Let's start with breakfast! Fiddlers, how about
some breakfast music!"

After royally entertaining the clan O'Sullivan, the king
regaled them with sacks of gold, coffers of jewels, and enough
food and drink to keep Crookhaven merry for months.

Then the O'Sullivans headed back to Crookhaven for the
real party.

Crookhaven was ready to celebrate, for the witch had come out of her snit. She and Kate both were in fine form as guests of honor at the big party. Seamus proudly served up his specialty—O'Sullivan stew. The townsfolk made sure that no one was left out by hanging a banner across the village green that read...

The next morning the witch came to Kate's door.

"I saw how you rode this horse," said the witch. "He likes you. He should be yours."

For once, Kate was tongue-tied.

"No one had ever done anything for me before you and your kin risked life and limb," the witch said. "It's so easy for folks to say how much they care, but who among us ever shows it? So it's my turn to show you. His name is Sebastian, and he'll serve you well. Just like his mother served me."

"But what's *your* name?" asked Kate.

"In the coven I was known as Blazing Dragon Whose Rage Has No Limits. But you can call me Fifi."

"Then for me, you'll always be *Aunt* Fifi," said Kate, and threw her arms around Aunt Fifi.

The following morning there was another knock on the door. The king entered, with flowers in his hand.

"Miss O'Sullivan, there is no one in my heart but you," he said. "Would you be my wife?"

Kate replied, "Oh, it's funny you should ask me today, Your Majesty. You see, I've just decided that after talking so much about the adventures of others it's time that I go find some of my own."

Kate led the king out the back door, where Sebastian stood, saddled and ready for a journey. She said her farewells to everyone and then mounted up.

"If your offer is still good in five years' time, you'll know where to find me," Kate called back to the king. "Just remember the way to Crookhaven."